The Great McGoniggle's Key Play

The Great McGoniggle's Key Play

by
SCOTT CORBETT

Illustrated by
Bill Ogden

An Atlantic Monthly Press Book
Little, Brown and Company
BOSTON   TORONTO

TEXT COPYRIGHT © 1976 BY SCOTT CORBETT

ILLUSTRATIONS COPYRIGHT © 1976 BY WILLIAM OGDEN

FIRST EDITION

T 04/76

Library of Congress Cataloging in Publication Data

Corbett, Scott.
    The Great McGoniggle's key play.

    "An Atlantic Monthly Press Book."
    SUMMARY: While collecting money for charity in front of a
supermarket, two boys become inadvertently involved in a jewel theft.
    [1. Mystery and detective stories] I. Ogden, William. II. Title.
PZ7.C79938Gu   [Fic]   75-38753
ISBN 0-316-15726-0

ATLANTIC-LITTLE, BROWN BOOKS
ARE PUBLISHED BY
LITTLE, BROWN AND COMPANY
IN ASSOCIATION WITH
THE ATLANTIC MONTHLY PRESS

*Published simultaneously in Canada
by Little, Brown & Company (Canada) Limited*

PRINTED IN THE UNITED STATES OF AMERICA

U. S. 1902442

For John Harvey Pierce III,
our first grandnephew

1

Ken Wetzel felt very foolish. Here he was in a football uniform standing in front of the Stop and Save supermarket shaking a collection can. Still, it was for a good cause. Every year, early in the fall, Hamilton City junior high school boys put on sports uniforms — football, baseball, soccer, whatever they played at school — and spent a Saturday afternoon collecting for the Jimmy Fund, which helped sick children.

"Jimmy Fund! Give to the Jimmy Fund! Thank you, ma'am," said Ken as an old lady dropped a coin into his can. It had a nice ring to it. Probably a quarter. He was doing all right. He and the Great McGoniggle had flipped to see who would get the supermarket for the first hour, and Ken had won.

People were pouring in and out of the store as if food had just been invented. Across the pedestrian mall, in front of the shopping center's other row of stores and shops, Mac was not doing as well. But no one could say he wasn't trying. Ken watched as Mac pointed his fingers like a gun at a man coming out of the camera store.

"Stick 'em up, mister! Your money or your life!"

The man grinned and put some money in his can. Mac was pretty smart about knowing which ones would respond to that kind of horseplay. Just then a police siren snarled in the distance. Mac cringed and crouched as if he were going to run.

"Gee, I didn't mean it!" he whined. "Don't turn me in!"

Mac loved to clown around and put on an act — "In my family we laugh so we won't cry," he had once remarked not quite jokingly. For that matter, there was a clownish look to Mac's face, with its tipped-up nose and wide mouth. Furthermore, Mac looked almost but not quite cross-eyed, and took a definitely cross-eyed view of the world. Life often became a nutty farce in which he played a starring role as the Great McGoniggle.

Ken had uneasy moments when he was with Mac, wondering what crazy thing he would say or do next. When he wasn't with him, Ken was uneasy, too, worrying about what he might be missing.

"Jimmy Fund! Give to the Jimmy Fund!" chanted Ken, rattling his can at a skinny young man who came hurrying across the mall. Ken tried everybody, even people who did not look like good prospects.

This man looked like trouble, complete with leather jacket, boots and aviator glasses. Ken expected not so much as a second glance, let alone any money.

The police car had turned in from the street and was weaving through the parking lot, quite close now. Seeing it coming, the young man stared around wildly. Then he saw Ken and one of his hands reached desperately into a pocket.

"Give to the Jimmy Fund, mister?" said Ken, holding out his can.

"Sure," said the man, and he really gave. He didn't just drop in a single coin, he put his hand over the top of the can and dropped in a fistful.

Plink! Plink! Plink! Plink! The last one hit with such a satisfying bump that Ken decided it must be at least a silver dollar.

"Gee, thanks!" It just proved how wrong he could be about givers.

"That's okay," said the man, and he seemed to feel better as he walked away.

He did not get far, however. With its siren growling, the police car eased onto the mall, scattering pedestrians. It pulled to the curb not ten feet from where Ken was standing. A policeman jumped out, a sergeant.

"Okay, Danny, get in."

"Huh?"

"We want to talk to you down at the station," said the sergeant, opening the rear door.

"What for? I ain't done nothing," said Danny, but he obeyed orders. The sergeant got in beside the driver and the car moved away, leaving Ken with his mouth open. Mac came galloping across the mall.

"What was that all about, Ken?"

"Search me! It was somebody called Danny, and he must be a crook. And he just gave me a whole fistful of change, too!"

"A regular Robin Hood. He wanted to do one last decent thing before they put him away," said Mac, rolling his eyes upward. Then he frowned. "Darn it, anyway! All the excitement, and I had to be on the wrong side of the mall."

2

Mac looked at his watch.

"Don't forget, in twenty minutes we change places!"

"Okay. Now get back to your post, McGoniggle, or I'll have to report you."

"Aye, aye, sir!" Mac saluted, did a clumsy about-face, and marched away on his storklike legs.

The hustle and bustle of the shopping center quickly returned to normal. Well-loaded wire grocery carts, pushed by weary shoppers, rattled down the ramp in the direction of the parking lot, where cars prowled for parking spaces. It was the busiest time of the day, and Ken did his best to make the most of it.

In exactly twenty minutes Mac was back again.

"Okay, Wetzel, I'm putting you on the bench," he said. Ken reluctantly changed places and moved over by the camera shop, the clothing store, and the delicatessen, where he found the pickings slimmer. Mac took his place and collected lots of money and had fun doing it.

Ken was always amazed that Mac could act as if he hadn't a care in the world. Mac had a father who was great about everything but holding a job and a mother who worked hard to keep things going for them all — including Mac's two older sisters and his kid brother. Nothing was secure for the McGoniggles, and yet they all seemed to enjoy life and each other to the full.

Nearly another hour had passed when for the second time that afternoon a car invaded the pedestrian mall, and this one was a hardtop sports car. Private cars were supposed to

stay off the mall. Nobody protested, maybe because the car stopped in front of Mac, and it looked almost as if the car had something to do with the Jimmy Fund. There were two men inside, both wearing dark glasses. One man beckoned to him. Mac stepped down beside the car.

Then the men drove off and Mac no longer had a can in his hand. Instead he had a bill in it and a jackpot-winner's expression on his face. He raced across the mall to report.

"Boy, that's the side where the action is, all right! Look at this!"

He was holding a twenty-dollar bill.

"Wow! Did those men give you that?"

"Yes! They gave it to me for my can!"

"What?"

"They did!"

"Why?"

"They said they wanted it for a souvenir."

"A souvenir? Aw, come on, now!"

"That's what they said! And I figured it

was a good deal for the fund, because there couldn't have been more than ten bucks in my can. It's nutty, but —"

"Nutty is right! Why would anyone want a Jimmy Fund can for a souvenir?"

"They said they wanted it because they used to shake cans for the fund when they were kids."

"Huh! I've heard of some crazy things people collect, but —"

"Well, who cares? It beats shrunken heads or used bubble gum. What a day!" said Mac with great satisfaction. "First a hoodlum is picked up by the cops, and then I sell my can for twenty smackers!"

"Wait a minute!" The two events suddenly linked up in Ken's mind in a startling way. "I was over there when . . ."

"Over where?"

"In front of the supermarket. And Danny put a whole bunch of — of something in my can . . ."

Mac blinked. Instantly he was on the same wavelength.

"You mean, maybe Danny put something in your can besides money?"

"Well? . . ."

"And those men wanted it! But by then we had changed sides, so they got the wrong can!"

They stared at each other, putting two and two together and finding the results excitingly sinister. The situation was made to order for the Great McGoniggle. He flung a finger aloft and spoke in a low voice charged with drama.

"Well, I'll tell you one thing, the sooner we have a look inside that can, the better!"

"What?" Ken glanced around them with a flustered expression, hoping none of the people passing by had heard this shameful suggestion. Pry open a Worthy Cause collection can? It simply wasn't done! "We can't fool around with —"

"Come on!"

"Come where?" said Ken as Mac dragged him away from his post. "We're supposed to stay here till five o'clock!"

"Never mind that; we've got more important things to do. What we need right now is a nice private hiding place where we can do the dirty work!"

3

A block down the street they came to a large billboard.

"Here, this will do," said Mac, and hauled Ken behind it. Ken was still protesting.

"Listen, we can't rip open a Jimmy Fund can —!"

"You're absolutely right!" agreed Mac with one of his crazy, crooked grins. "And we won't have to. Watch!"

Pulling off his football helmet, he squatted on his haunches, set the helmet upside down on the ground, and began shaking the contents of the can into it. The slot in the top of the can was a big wide one, which made the job easy.

"Well . . . that's just as bad!" Squatting beside him, Ken was glancing in all directions, a bundle of nerves. "If anyone sees us, we're done for!"

"Schoolboys Rob Jimmy Fund Can," declared Mac, as though he were reading a newspaper headline. "What's the world coming to? I tell you, kids today are a rotten bunch!" A stream of nickels and dimes rained into the helmet.

"Well, it's nothing to laugh about!"

"Don't worry, nobody's going to see us. Who runs around looking behind billboards? And we won't be here long — There!"

Something that was not money fell into the helmet. Mac's fingers pounced on the object and brought it out.

"A key!"

It was an odd-looking key with a number on it.

"What kind of key is that?" Ken wondered.

The jackpot-winner's expression was back on Mac's face.

"Happy days! All those trips down to the bus station to pick up Aunt Glenda every time she comes for the weekend — they've finally paid off!"

Ken wanted to hit him. In fact, he did. "What are you talking about, darn it?"

"I told you. Just about every other week we drive down there to meet her bus from Scrantonville. Sometimes the bus is late and we have to wait around. I know every inch of that bus station, and I know a key like this when I see one."

"Well, what for crying out loud *is* it?"

"You know the kind of lockers they have for luggage? You set your bags inside, then you put a quarter in the slot and shut the door and turn the key. The key won't come out of the lock until you've put in the quarter. Then you can turn the key, lock the box, and take the key out."

"Well, sure, I know —"

"Okay. When you come back and unlock

22

the door to take out your bags, the key stays in the lock. It won't lock the box and come out again till another quarter is put into the slot."

Mac held up the key. "Well, this is one of those!"

So he was smart enough to figure out what kind of key it was. Ken wished he had thought of it, so he had to argue.

"Yes, but that doesn't mean it's from the bus station," he scoffed. "They've got lockers like that lots of places. The railroad station, the airport — and they're all alike. Why, it could even be from a locker in some other city!"

"Maybe so, but I'll bet they're not all *that* close to being the same, and this one looks like the bus station kind to me."

"Sure — because you *want* it to be," said Ken, but Mac ignored him. He was staring thoughtfully at the key.

"Now, why did Danny Boy drop it in your can? . . ."

"That's easy. He saw the cops coming, and had to get rid of it."

"Right," said Mac. "If they found it on him, they'd check it out and locate whatever he has stashed in the locker."

"And when they took him in, he got word to his pals somehow about what he had done with the key, and they came after it."

"Sure! Or his pals saw him drop the key in your can."

"Okay, then, let's get going!" Ken was the son of a successful lawyer. He clearly saw their proper course of action. "We've got to take this straight to the police station and —"

"Hold it," said Mac. "I've been thinking. One of my favorite people is the old cop who's always on duty Saturday at the bus station. I've known him since I was this high," he added, holding his hand out beside him, which put it about a foot above the ground.

"What's he got to do with it?"

"Well, we're great buddies. Officer Kringle,

his name is — he always told me his first name is Kris, and he looks like it could be. He's a great old guy. If there *is* something funny going on here, and there's anything important hidden in that locker, I want him to get part of the credit for finding it."

"*If* it's in the bus station."

"Well, even if it isn't, we can at least show him the key and let him take it from there. It beats walking into a police station and talking to a lot of strange cops, who probably won't even take us seriously."

There was some logic to that. Offbeat logic typical of Mac, but logic all the same. Ken felt himself slipping.

"We could call my father —" he began, but broke off as he remembered that his father was out of town on a case. They were on their own. "No, he's not here. Well . . . all right, but let's get that money back in the can before somebody comes along and sees us!"

"We need some of it for operating expenses," said Mac, busily counting out a handful of change. "Got to get to the bus station. We can put it back later."

Ken groaned.

"Well, okay, but hurry up!"

"What a time to have no pockets!" grumbled Mac, looking down at his football pants. "Well, I'll just put it in with the twenty," he said, and poured the coins into the neck of his jersey. As he did, Ken gasped. He was sure he heard shuffling footsteps on the other side of the billboard.

"Someone's coming!" he hissed.

Mac threw up his hands.

"All is lost!" he cried. "We've had it!"

A long, broad nose appeared around the corner of the billboard — the nose of a golden retriever. He looked them over, wagged his tail, and disappeared again. Mac snickered.

"Don't you know a dog when you hear one, Ken?"

"Not that time!" Ken was limp. "I thought . . . I don't know what I thought."

Mac sighed.

"Wetzel, I'm afraid you're not cut out for a life of crime," he said, and dribbled the rest of the money back into the can, using one hand as a funnel. Then he jammed his football helmet back on his head. "Let's go!"

With Mac in the lead, jingling at every step, they slipped out from behind the billboard and hurried toward the next intersection.

"You sound like a slot machine!" complained Ken. "Come on, let's cross over."

"Why?"

"Well, the bus stop is across the street —"

"Bus stop? We can't wait around for any buses! We've got to get a move on and — Happy days! We're in luck!"

Once again the Great McGoniggle flung a finger aloft, but this time it was a commanding finger, and this time he cried, "Taxi!"

4

The cab pulled to the curb and stopped. The driver leaned across the front seat to glare out at Mac.

"Who are you kidding?"

"We're not kidding," said Mac, pulling open the rear door. "We want to go to the bus station."

"What? Get out of here!" yelled the driver as they climbed in. "If you think I'm handing out free rides to a couple of schoolkids —"

"Don't worry; we can pay," said Mac, reaching into the neck of his jersey and pawing around inside it.

"Show me!" jeered the driver.

Mac flicked a bill into sight.

"Got change for a twenty?"

The driver's eyes bugged at the bill, but before he could sputter a reply, Mac had put it away and dug out a handful of coins, which he proceeded to count.

"Buck fifty . . . seventy-five . . . two . . . I got it all! Never mind the bill, here's some change, two bucks' worth. That ought to do it. You can give me what's left when we get there," he said, handing it over and settling back in his seat as though taxicabs were an everyday thing in his life.

The driver looked at the money in his hand and turned to the wheel, shaking his head.

"You kids today!" he said bitterly as they drove off. "You get money handed to you on a silver platter. The idea of a couple of squirts like you riding around in taxicabs! And what are you doing with all that dough anyway?"

Mac held up Ken's can and rattled it.

"I suppose you think we took it from the Jimmy Fund," he said sorrowfully.

The driver glared at them in his mirror. "No, you don't look that rotten," he said grudgingly, "but I still say you ought to darn well walk or take a bus, the way *I* did when *I* was a boy!"

"We're in a hurry."

"Everybody's in a big hurry these days," snapped the driver, and fell into a grumpy silence as he concentrated on making it to the bus station and getting rid of them. Mac glanced at Ken and dug an elbow into his ribs. Ken rolled his eyes and stared out the window, not knowing whether to laugh or hit Mac. Life with the Great McGoniggle got that way sometimes.

After a while they were both watching the meter, which was whirling up ten cents more and ten cents more at a terrible rate.

"You ought to be rich, mister," said Mac.

"Wanna get out and walk?"

"No, thanks. Not till it hits two bucks' worth, anyway."

"Is that all you took — is that all you brought with you?" asked Ken, correcting himself hastily.

"That's all the small change, yes — and it's too bad, too, because I had my hands on plenty more. Oh, I do wish Daddy would stop giving me my allowance in twenty-dollar bills; it's such a nuisance," said Mac, enjoying the deepening color of the driver's red neck.

When they pulled up in front of the bus station the meter read, "$1.90." U. S. 1902442

"Wow! That was close. Keep the change," said Mac with a flourish of his hand.

The driver held up a dime sarcastically. "All of it?"

"Unless you'd like to contribute to the Jimmy Fund," said Mac, shoving the can under his nose. The driver sighed and made his contribution.

"Man, did I ever come out on the short end of *this* deal!" he grumbled.

"That reminds me, I haven't given anything myself yet," said Mac, and made the driver's eyes bug again as he grandly stuffed the twenty-dollar bill through the slot. "Thanks for the ride! Come, Kenneth, we must be going!"

5

The boys jumped out, and some other passengers stepped in. The driver escaped, leaving Mac and Ken standing among a crowd of people. They had been too busy paying the cab driver to notice the crowd and the two police cars and an ambulance at the curb.

"Hey!" Mac grabbed Ken's arm. "What's that all about?"

They joined the onlookers and a man was delighted to tell them what had happened.

"See that office on the third floor, Berman Jewelry Company? A couple of punks with stockings pulled over their heads got in there and held up old man Berman. Hit him on the head, took a bunch of diamond rings, and left him tied up. It's lucky somebody happened to go in and find him there before the building closed or he'd have been there till Monday morning."

Ken and Mac stared up at the Berman Jewelry Company window, then stared at each other, and then stared over their shoulders at the bus station. Mac's fingers tightened on Ken's arm.

"Say! You don't suppose . . . ?"

"You mean, maybe Danny —"

"Yes! What if he was one of the two punks who stole the jewelry? He could have brought the stuff across the street here to the bus station —"

"Stashed it in a locker —"

"And been free and clear! Come on, let's find Kringle!"

They rushed in the bus station door and into a boy in a baseball uniform with a Jimmy Fund can in his hand.

"Hi!" he said. "You're early!"

"We're not here to take over for you; we're on a special project," said Mac. "Listen, have you seen a cop around here?"

"Lots of them, but they're all across the street. Somebody stuck up a jewelry store —"

"We know. But I'm looking for the cop that works here in the station. Fat man with white hair."

"Oh, him. Sure, I was talking to him, but I haven't seen him around lately."

"Okay. Come on, Ken," said Mac, and darted away toward the information desk. A bored-looking woman was sitting behind it filing her nails.

"Hi, Mrs. Shamblin!"

She glanced up and stopped looking so bored.

"Well, hi, Mac," she said.

"We're looking for Officer Kringle. Do you know where he is?"

"Across the street somewhere, I guess. He

went over to see if there was something he could do. I expect he'll be back soon, though."

"Well . . . we'll wait. Thanks, Mrs. Shamblin." Mac walked away, complaining to Ken, "Just our luck!"

"Well, we might know he'd check in over there. We could go look for him, and if we don't find him, we could tell one of the other cops — there's plenty of them over there!"

"No, wait, I just thought of something." Mac was glancing around. "Before we do anything else, let's go look at the lockers and see if I'm right about the key being from here."

"Good idea! Where are they?"

"There."

Mac pointed toward a corridor that led to a side entrance. Both walls were lined with metal storage lockers. Only the few lockers that were not being used had their keys in their locks. Mac took out the key they had found and held it alongside the handle of one of those keys.

"See?" His eyes glinted with triumph. "Same kind of numbers. Now let's look for Number Thirty."

Number 30 was on the lefthand side, bottom row, halfway down the corridor. And it had no key in it.

"There! That proves it!" crowed Mac.

But something perverse and negative in Ken's makeup made him resist Mac's cocksure attitude.

"The heck it does!" he retorted stubbornly. "It still doesn't prove it's *our* Number Thirty, just because the key is gone."

Mac cast a wary glance around the corridor. A woman came through carrying a suitcase in one hand and dragging a little girl by the other.

"Hurry or we'll miss our bus!"

A man reading a newspaper walked slowly past, holding the paper so high it hid his dark glasses. Two teenagers went past with transistor radios jammed against their ears.

"What are you going to do?" asked Ken.

"Try the key."

"*What?*"

"I'll just slip it in to see if it fits, that's all," said Mac, squatting down to the level of the locker door. "I won't open it."

"Don't do that!" said Ken, quickly squatting down beside him. "Wait till your friend comes back!"

"I tell you, I won't open it!" insisted Mac, slipping the key into the keyhole. "I just want to check. . . ."

It went in smoothly. He beamed at Ken in his crisscrossed way.

"See? It fits!"

"Aw, for Pete's sake, Mac! Probably any of these keys will slip into any of the keyholes — but that doesn't mean they're the right one for that lock. That doesn't prove they'll turn it and open it. . . ."

Even while he was saying what he said, Ken had a funny feeling he was making a big mistake. When it was too late, he realized he was simply setting up a challenge the Great McGoniggle could not resist.

And Mac could not. A gleam came into his eyes, and his wrist made a quarter-turn.

The key clicked in the lock.

"Hey!"

"Omigosh!"

"You opened it!"

The door opened a crack. Mac opened it another inch or two and peered inside. Then he hastily slammed the door and held it shut. He was breathing hard.

"There's a big flat leather case in there! I'll bet it's the diamonds!" he whispered in a hoarse voice. "We've got to lock them up again! Quick, shake a quarter out of your can!"

"What? How can I shake money out of a Jimmy Fund can right here where everybody can see us?"

Ken didn't have to face that problem.

Suddenly a powerful push sent him sprawling on the floor. At the same instant Mac tumbled in the other direction.

"What are you kids doing in my locker?"

The man who snarled this question was wearing dark glasses. He snatched the leather case out of the locker and turned to run down the corridor.

"Let's get him, Ken!"

Ken scrambled to his feet. He and Mac were dressed for the occasion. They were not great football players, but they hit Dark Glasses with the two best tackles of their athletic careers. As the man came down, he fumbled. The leather case went flying, hit the wall, and sprang open, and the air glittered. A man who looked like a beardless Santa Claus in the wrong uniform waddled through the entrance at the end of the corridor, took one look, and came a-running.

"What's going on here?" Officer Kringle demanded, and knocked the rest of the wind

out of Dark Glasses by dropping to his knees on top of him.

"Look!" Mac pointed to the merchandise scattered all over the floor.

"Well, I'll be — Pick up those rings, boys!" cried Officer Kringle. "They're evidence!"

6

"Word about the robbery had just gone out over the police radio to the cars," Officer Kringle explained to the boys sometime later. "Sergeant Lanza was riding around and spotted Danny and knew he was the kind who ought to be pulled in for questioning."

"And Danny couldn't let them find that key on him," said Mac.

"You bet he couldn't. They'd have frisked him as a matter of routine, and the minute they found that key his goose would have been cooked. When he saw them coming he had to act fast. So he dropped the key in your can. Then, when they took him in to the police station, right away he called his lawyer.

The lawyer came over, and through him Danny got word about the key to his buddies.

"They jumped in a car and went for the can, but they got the wrong one. So then one of them, Jo-Jo, went to the bus station and hung around, trying to figure how he could bust into that locker. When you showed up, Jo-Jo saw his chance, and he might have made it if you hadn't nailed him. You kids are going to grow up to be a couple of football stars, if you ask me!"

"Aw, we're not so hot; we're just second string," said Ken.

"That so? Good thing you weren't first string or you'd have broken Jo-Jo in two! What position do you play, Mac?"

"Left tackle."

"How about you, Ken?"

"Right tackle."

"Hmm. Well, it figures."

The Sunday paper carried a picture of Mac and Ken and Officer Kringle accepting a check for the Jimmy Fund from Mr. Berman, who was lying in a hospital bed with a bandage around his head, but enjoying a big cigar.

After thinking it over, Mac declared, "You know, there's only one other thing I could wish for."

"What's that?" asked Ken.

"I wish I could have seen that cab driver's face when he opened his Sunday paper and saw our picture!"

Books by Scott Corbett

The Trick Books

THE LEMONADE TRICK
THE MAILBOX TRICK
THE DISAPPEARING DOG TRICK
THE LIMERICK TRICK
THE BASEBALL TRICK
THE TURNABOUT TRICK
THE HAIRY HORROR TRICK
THE HATEFUL PLATEFUL TRICK
THE HOME RUN TRICK
THE HOCKEY TRICK
THE BLACK MASK TRICK

What Makes It Work?

WHAT MAKES A CAR GO?
WHAT MAKES A TV WORK?
WHAT MAKES A LIGHT GO ON?
WHAT MAKES A PLANE FLY?
WHAT MAKES A BOAT FLOAT?

Easy-to-Read Adventure Stories

DR. MERLIN'S MAGIC SHOP
THE GREAT CUSTARD PIE PANIC
THE BOY WHO WALKED ON AIR
THE GREAT McGONIGGLE'S GRAY GHOST
THE GREAT McGONIGGLE'S KEY PLAY

Suspense Stories

TREE HOUSE ISLAND
DEAD MAN'S LIGHT
CUTLASS ISLAND
COP'S KID
THE BASEBALL BARGAIN
THE MYSTERY MAN
THE CASE OF THE GONE GOOSE
THE CASE OF THE FUGITIVE FIREBUG
THE CASE OF THE TICKLISH TOOTH
THE RED ROOM RIDDLE
DEAD BEFORE DOCKING
RUN FOR THE MONEY
HERE LIES THE BODY
THE CASE OF THE SILVER SKULL
THE CASE OF THE BURGLED BLESSING BOX